"So, you're training Callie to be Gammy's eyes?"

Jake nodded. "Myrna could live independently for years to come." Maintaining Myrna's independence was Jake's goal.

"What if I take over as Callie's Puppy Raiser? Then she could get used to living with Gammy."

Jake hadn't expected this. "Do you like dogs? I don't require my foster parents to have experience training, but they must have a love for dogs."

"Who doesn't love puppies?" Olivia smiled. "I've taken a sabbatical from my job with no set return date, so I can stay as long as it takes to get Callie trained. By then, I'll be able to better assess whether it's in my grandmother's best interest to stay in Bluebell or move to Miami and live with me."

Didn't Myrna get a say in the matter? Of course, that was between Olivia and her grandmother. "Okay then." He extended his hand. "It's a deal. We'll work together to get Callie trained if you agree to hold off on any decision about moving Myrna."

Weekdays, **Jill Weatherholt** works for the City of Charlotte. On the weekend, she writes contemporary stories about love, faith and forgiveness. Raised in the suburbs of Washington, DC, she now resides in North Carolina. She holds a degree in psychology from George Mason University and a paralegal studies certification from Duke University. She shares her life with her real-life hero and number one supporter. Jill loves connecting with readers at jillweatherholt.com.

Books by Jill Weatherholt

Love Inspired

Second Chance Romance
A Father for Bella
A Mother for His Twins
A Home for Her Daughter
A Dream of Family
Searching for Home
Their Inseparable Bond

Visit the Author Profile page at LoveInspired.com.